THE MONSTER GANG

Felicity Everett
Adapted by Gill Harvey

Illustrated by Teri Gower

Reading Consultant: Alison Kelly
Roehampton University of Surrey

Contents

Chapter 1

One rainy Saturday

Micky + Ben when we went to the beach

Ruby on her skates

Tas pulling faces

Micky, Lee + all their comics

Me + Goldie

It was too wet to play outside, so Ellie was looking at her photo album.

At last, the rain stopped. As Ellie went out, Tas zoomed up on her bike.

"Ben, Lee and Micky are on their way," Tas added.

Stop splashing!

Come on, Ben!

"They're slow because Ben's wearing his new boots."

Just then, Ruby spun past. She was learning how to do cartwheels.

Look! I've got the hang of it now.

"Hi Ellie! Hi Tas!" she said. "What are you doing?"

Ellie felt a plop of something wet on her cheek. She sighed. It was raining again.

"Looks like we're going inside," she said.

Do you want to come to my room?

Chapter 2

A great idea!

In Ellie's room, they lay
around. They played games...

...they drew pictures of space men and monstrous aliens...

...they played more games...

I spy with my little eye...

...then they were bored.

It was still raining outside.
There was nothing left to do...

...until Ben had a fantastic idea.

Let's start a gang!

Chapter 3

The new gang

"A gang needs a good name," said Ellie.

They each tried to think of one. It was tricky. But, in the end, everyone had an idea.

They wrote their ideas on
pieces of paper.

Then they folded the papers
up and put them into Tas's
bike helmet.

"You pick one out, Ben," said Lee. "The gang was your idea."

Ben closed his eyes and put his hand into the helmet. He swirled it around the papers... dug deep... and fished one out.

Ben read what was on the
paper. "The Monster Gang!"
he said. He looked very pleased
with himself.

I've picked
my own idea!

Everyone agreed it was a
perfect name.

"What do Monster Gangs do?" asked Ruby.

"They look scary," said Lee.

"We'll have to dress up!" cried Ellie.

"Gangs need a place to meet," said Micky. "And monsters need a den... I know! My grandad's got a treehouse. How about that?"

Let's all meet tomorrow morning.

A treehouse was a great den. Now, they were a real gang.

Chapter 4

The first meeting

The next morning, six
monsters clambered
into the treehouse.

It was hard to tell who
was who.

The treehouse hadn't been used for ages. Inside, it was covered in dust. And it didn't look much like a monster den.

So, they drew scary pictures.

They made creepy bats out of paper and cobwebs out of string.

"I know how to make scary spiders," said the spotty blue monster. "Look!"

Then they stuck everything up. It took ages to pin up the cobwebs.

"Whew!" said the green
monster. "That was hard
work. I'm hungry now."

Luckily, two of the gang
had brought monsterish food to
eat. They had a monster feast!
The monsters munched away.

Then the blue monster, who was Ben, decided to find out who the other monsters were.

As he handed out drinks, he started to guess.

Ah! Scraped knees...

Ruby's bruises gave her away.

"Is this hair real?" asked Ben. He gave it a tug, just to be sure.

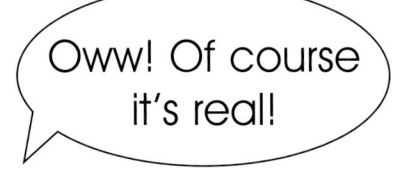

Oww! Of course it's real!

"Sorry, Tas," said Ben. "I didn't mean to hurt you."

27

Micky was easy to guess. He couldn't see without his glasses and had to wear them over his costume.

"I'd know those glasses anywhere," said Ben.

The red monster had a comic poking out of his back pocket.

A comic...
that could be Micky
or Lee...

Ben didn't really need a clue, with Lee's face grinning at him.

"That just leaves one," said
Ben. The last monster smiled
down from the tree, and
reached for a drink.

"You must be Ellie," said Ben.
"There's no one else left."

"Come on down, Ellie," said Ruby. "Let's take a closer look at your costume."

It doesn't *look* much like Ellie...

Chapter 5

A perfect disguise

The monster climbed down
from the tree. Tas pulled her
ear to make her mask move.
But it stayed firmly in place.

Micky got down on his hands and knees to inspect the monster's feet.

Hmmm... the nails look real...

How did you put it on?

"It must be an all-in-one suit," said Ruby. "It's great!"

They all decided that Ellie's costume was the best.

It's fantastic, Ellie!

Everyone agreed that she should be their gang leader. After all, Ellie was the only one who looked like a real monster.

They made her a Monster Gang Leader badge. She grinned and ate a chocolate muffin to celebrate.

Chapter 6

Gang business

Now they had a leader, they needed a secret sign. They tried lots of different ones.

Too silly...

...too hard...

...too rude...

But this one was just right.

"Gangs need rules," said Micky. "Let's make some up."

Making up the rules was fun.
Their gang leader wrote them
down, eating another muffin.

Just then, they heard a
voice. A voice they all knew!

Chapter 7

Who's there?

"It can't be Ellie," said Ben.
"She's already here. She's our
gang leader!"

They rushed to the door to peer down from the treehouse.

It was Ellie... with her dog, Goldie, wagging his tail by her side.

The rest of the gang stared at her. How could she be in two places at once?

Sorry I'm late! I had to take Goldie for a walk.

They scrambled back into the treehouse. Ellie hurried after them. But their gang leader had vanished.

"Look! There's a note," said Ellie. She picked it up. "Oh... it doesn't make sense."

Ruby guessed how to read the note. "It's mirror writing!" she said.

When they held the note up to a mirror, everything became clear.

Did you guess my secret? I'm a real monster! I hope I can come to the next meeting of the Monster Gang.

Love
Ug
XXX

Try these other books in
Series One:

The Burglar's Breakfast: Alfie Briggs is a burglar. After a hard night's thieving, he likes to go home to a tasty meal. But one day he gets back to discover someone has stolen his breakfast!

The Dinosaurs Next Door: Stan loves living next door to Mr. Puff. His house is full of amazing things. Best of all are the dinosaur eggs — until they begin to hatch...

Series editor: Lesley Sims

Designed by
Maria Wheatley and
Katarina Dragoslavić

This edition first published in 2007 by Usborne Publishing Ltd.,
Usborne House, 83-85 Saffron Hill, London EC1N 8RT, England.
www.usborne.com Copyright © 2007, 2002, 1995, 1994
Usborne Publishing Ltd.